Hyst‹

Winning short stories, flasl
Hysteria 2022 W...

Edited by Linda Parkinson-Hardman

Hysteria 9

Copyright ©2022, Linda Parkinson-Hardman

All rights reserved. The right of the individual contributors to be identified as the author of their work has been asserted in accordance with the Copyright, Designs and Patents Act 1988.

No paragraph of this publication may be reproduced, copied or transmitted save with written permission or in accordance with the provisions of the Copyright, Designs and Patents Act 1988, or under the terms of any license, permitting limited copying issued by the Copyright Licensing Agency, 33 Alfred Place, London, WC1E 7DP.

Any person who does any unauthorised act in relation to this publication may be liable to criminal prosecution and civil claims for damages.

Published by: Crystal Clear Books

ISBN: 978-1-387-44773-2

Website: www.hysteriawc.co.uk

All characters in this publication are fictitious and any resemblance to real persons, living or dead is purely coincidental.

Cover Image: © Andreas Lischka from Pixabay

ABOUT THE HYSTERIA WRITING COMPETITION

Hysteria is an annual, international writing competition. It opens on the 1st of April each year and closes at midnight on the 31st August. You can find out more about the competition, including rules and guidelines for entries on the website: *www.hysteriawc.co.uk*.

Dedication

The competition and this anthology wouldn't have been possible without the support and help of a wonderful team of readers and this year's writer in residence:

Diane Jackman, Gillian Scholey, Richard Teague, Rachel Angel, Steven Patchett, Lindy Newns, Jill Sinclair, Vishaal Pathak, Yvonne James, Eithne Cullen, Kate Franklin, El Rhodes.

Foreword

I am fascinated by the way words and language can be used in such a multitude of ways to invoke a sense of space, place, scenario or persona. Each year I'm blown away by the quality of the stories and poetry that emerges from the creative imagination of so many people, and this year is no exception.

When I was thinking about a theme for the year I looked up the meaning of the word Peace and was treated to the following meanings:

1. The absence of war or other hostilities.

2. An agreement or a treaty to end hostilities: negotiated the peace.

3. Freedom from quarrels and disagreement; harmonious relations: roommates living in peace with each other.

4. Public security and order: was arrested for disturbing the peace.

5. Inner contentment; serenity: peace of mind.

As it happens, the majority of entries focused on harmonious relations, freedom from quarrels and disagreement and significantly, inner contentement; serenity and peace of mind. These are the meanings that were uppermost in my mind when I eventually set the theme.

To be honest I was a little concerned at the beginning that too many entries would relate to the absence of war given this topic has dominated the news for much of the year. So it was with much relief that where war was a source of inspiration it didn't dominate.

All the finalists deserve to have their entries read again and again as I believe they have the power to help our species navigate away from a sense of constant conflict towards the real peace that is available when we recognise we are all one.

Linda

Contents

ABOUT THE HYSTERIA WRITING COMPETITION	3
FOREWORD	4
ADVICE FOR ENTRANTS	8
FLASH FICTION	11
AT PEACE WITH MYSELF IN THE MIDST OF THE CHAOS OF HALF STARTED PROJECTS	12
THE HEALING POWER OF SALT	14
THE PRAYER OF ANNELIESE MÜLLER	16
DISTURBING THE PEACE	18
SENNEN COVE	20
THE WOMAN WHO DROPPED A STITCH	22
PAIN AND ABLE	24
A BIT OF A PICKLE	26
A SIMPLE HAREM OF SEALS	28
MESSAGE FROM THE SEA OF TRANQUILITY	30
POETRY	32
GIRL IN A CATHEDRAL	33
A DROP OF PEACE	34
FINDING PEACE AT THE BOTTOM OF THE BUCKET	36
A NUN'S REFLECTION	38
RIVER	40
PEACE OFFERING	41
300789	42
UNSPOKEN	43

LESSONS	45
WITHHELD VOICE	46
SHORT STORIES	48
ET IN ARCADIA EGO	49
PEACE ON THE NORTHERN LINE	53
FLIGHTS OF FANCY	56
AT THE END OF THE DAY	60
REST IN PEACE	64
IN PURSUIT OF PEACE	68
A PEACE OF CHOCOLATE	73
WHO ARE THE WITCHES	78
AN ABSTRACT PEACE	82
CATCHING MY BREATH	86

Advice for Entrants

Reader's Advice for Entrants from Rachel Angel

Well done to everyone who entered this year's Hysteria competition. It was wonderful to read so many different interpretations of the theme, 'peace'.

I felt that the entries that stood out the most to me were those with characters that really made me feel something for what they were experiencing, entries that balanced sadness and humour, those that used the senses, and those where dialogue moved the story on well.

Once you have finished writing, I would advise you to check, check and check again! Check the competition rules and ensure that your entry meets them all. Put your piece away for a few days. Read it out aloud again - does it flow well? Are there any parts that stall and need further work? Is it well-presented? Are all words spelt correctly?

Thank you to all the entrants for giving me the opportunity to read your work. I thoroughly enjoyed reading the entries for the short story section and found a few emotional ones that will stay with me for some time.

Congratulations to all the writers published in the Hysteria 9 anthology.

Rachel Angel is currently studying for a master's degree in Creative Writing with the Open University.

Readers Advice for Entrants from Jill Sinclair

The standard of submissions for Flash Fiction was very high. I was hugely impressed by the originality, inventiveness and breadth of ideas.

If I had one criticism it would be the repetition of words.

There are so many words to choose from! Unless word repetition is used for effect, to create rhythm or as a deliberate motif or linking device, it feels lazy to use the same word twice in such a short space. So I would urge writers to read and re-read their work and if a word appears more than once ask 'why is that?' If there's no good reason, find another word.

> Jill has always written – some fiction, but mostly reviews, profiles and features for newspapers and magazines. She has had one non-fiction book published on the 'Art of Being ill - How to be a Better Patient' and is an enthusiastic reader of short stories and flash fiction.

Readers Advice from Diane Jackman

Do you remember school exam time, the teacher saying "Read the Question" in as many ways as she could? And still the tendency was to let your eye fall on the paper, pick out a few familiar words, and think, "Yes, I know what this is about." We all do it. But it can be the fatal error when entering a writing competition. When is the closing date? What time on the closing date? I've been caught out by that myself, polishing a poem at 8pm on the last day, only to discover entries had to be in by 5pm. Is there a theme? How many words or lines? If the competition states 40 lines of poetry, the judges won't stop to read your line by line response to Hiawatha. If they want 12 lines, you won't get away with a sonnet. Is it unpublished?

The rules surrounding websites, poetry groups, workshops are as many and various as the competitions. Read these rules very carefully. It seems so basic, and yet many good pieces of writing sink without trace because the writer has not read the rules with sufficient care.

Judging the poetry competition is always a joy. If there isn't a theme, then the world is your oyster and poems fly in from so many different angles, sometimes making it difficult to judge. Where there is a theme, there may be occasions when similar takes on the selected word appear in different poems. If the imaginative idea is almost repeated, the judge has to work on the quality of the language and imagery. The poems which stand out for me are the ones where the theme is not taken too literally; where the poet has stretched their imagination and stepped beyond the theme to tell a story which illustrates, but does not simply describe.

Diane Jackman's poetry has appeared in small press magazines and anthologies and has won or placed in several competitions. Starting as a published children's writer she now concentrates on poetry. And her first collection Lessons from the Orchard is due out this summer from Sacred Eagle Publishing Ltd. She is passionately interested in medieval rabbit warrens and Anglo-Saxon literature. She has now led poetry workshops and also runs a poetry café in Brandon in the heart of Breckland, England's desert. You can meet her on her website here: www.dianejackman.co.uk

FLASH FICTION

The Flash Fiction category is open to entries with a maximum word count of 250 words. These ultra-short stories needed to be complete and give the reader the satisfaction of not being left hanging.

Flash fiction is fictional work of extreme brevity that still offers the author and reader the benefit of character and plot development.

AT PEACE WITH MYSELF IN THE MIDST OF THE CHAOS OF HALF STARTED PROJECTS

Caroline Jenner

The ironing board hovers alongside the overflowing clothes basket, half hidden by a parlour plant. Triffid like, as if planning their escape, waxy leaves spread across the growing piles of mending. An ancient, red jumper, which may or may not be going to a charity shop, sits alongside piles of notebooks, some filled, some half started, teetering precariously on the chest of drawers. Bead and button boxes sit expectantly, waiting to be opened. A lifetime's supply of wool tumbles out from behind a full length mirror: brilliant colours; a rainbow of textures; my fingers itch to begin new projects.

At the end of the bed odd, unpaired socks ingratiate themselves with each. The distant hum of traffic interrupted occasionally by a magpie's squawk, the click of a distant computer, the scratch of my pen; a patchwork of sounds wallpapering my room. Standing sentry, the fan is a reminder of hot sunny days as we slip quietly into Autumn.

A cross stitch of the Last Supper, barely started, encircled by its wooden hoop, prods a guilty thought of a promise made last year to make a fresh start, complete projects, tidy up. The pink satchel, full of sheet music, peers accusingly at me – a reminder of another interest pushed onto a back burner.

My pen scratches across the page – before me on the bed my hand touches fur, the peaceful breathing of a contented tabby. Everything can wait, this is my time to write.

Caroline Jenner, retired English teacher, and would be short story writer, lives in South London. She particularly enjoys the challenge of micro fiction and exploring the concise nature of a complete story in a few words. Her work has been published by Free Flash Fiction, Sweetycat Press and Pure Slush. She has been longlisted for the Retreat West Monthly Micro Fiction Competition, and shortlisted for Globe Soup, Cranked Anvil, Writers Magazine, Secret Attic and in 2021 came second in the Hastings Writing Room Two Halves Flash Fiction Competition.

carolinejenner@carolinejenner3

THE HEALING POWER OF SALT

Caroline Beuley

We are whitecaps that crown the waves, rolling towards our own dissolution. Rising, cresting, shattering in an endless pattern that varies only in amplitude and endpoint. Before we tumbled particulate across the ocean floor, we were something else. Girls, figs, tigers. One of us was a conch shell. Now, we are this. Now, we are at peace. Though we break upon the shore, we will never break again.

It is late afternoon. The tide is high. We dissolve upon the white sand of a desolate beach. As we drag backwards from the shore, dancing with loose shells, two figures crest the dune. But we are withdrawing, and soon we are pulled under, and there is only deep green. When we rise again, slipping from sea to surface, we see the couple clearly. They are lying on the beach now, wrapped in each other. Water susurates below us as we rush to them.

Something stirs in me - a drop in a placid tidal pool, disturbing long-dormant dirt. The couple rolls on the sand. Their toes intertwine. I long to touch them.

I do. I wash over their feet. In their toes and ankles is the warm, insistent pulse of love. I remember a set of ten, tiny toes. The couple shrieks with mirth, hitching their legs away, clasping hands. In their clasped hands is the prayer for love's eternity. I wish them better luck than me.

I slip backwards.. The tide is ebbing, losing ground. I lose myself in it.

Caroline Beuley is a writer and high school English teacher based in Washington, D.C. Caroline has taken courses in Fiction Writing at American University in Paris and Oxford University. Caroline has had fiction published or forthcoming in Flash Fiction Magazine, Women on Writing, Spaceports & Spidersilk, Maudlin House, and Schlock! Webzine as well as comedy writing published in Belladonna, The Weekly Humorist, and Points-in-Case. When she's not teaching or writing, she enjoys reading, taking her dachshund, Dumbledore, on walks, and throwing bits of paper around for her cat, Eloise.

https://carolinebeuley.com/

THE PRAYER OF ANNELIESE MÜLLER

Chris Cotham

Spring

I pray we will dig our marriage bed deep, aerating its soil and raking out tangles; that I will bloom with the fruit of a single seedling; that this will sprout as we feed and fertilise; that we'll plant out, pollinate again, and propagate anew until our well runs dry.

Summer

I pray we will nurture and nourish, hedge and stake, trim and train; that we'll graft and they'll grow; that, potted on, they'll flourish, watered regularly, weeded weekly, and pruned with a care which will hurt us far more than it hurts them.

Autumn

I pray we will never cross-fertilise or bed out; that, when our perennials uproot themselves and winter threatens, we'll trim our love to its roots, earth-up our once blossom-soft bed, and mulch down side by side, waiting for a spring we know will come, but shall not see.

Chris Cottom lives near Macclesfield, England, and once wrote insurance words. He won the 2021 Retreat West Flash Fiction Prize and was the people's choice winner of the 2022 LoveReading Very Short Story Award. He's also been published by Anansi Archive, Apricot Press, Bournemouth Writing Prize, Cranked Anvil, London Lit Lab, National Flash Fiction Day, On The Premises, Parracombe Prize,

Shooter Flash, Story Nook, Streetcake, and The Centifictionist; and broadcast on BBC Radio Leeds. In the early 1970s he lived next door to JRR Tolkien.

DISTURBING THE PEACE

Tracy Davidson

I didn't like the new people upstairs. They shouted, played techno music past midnight, held raucous parties. And they couldn't walk quietly across floors, instead they thundered about like stampeding elephants.

Anyone who complained got subjected to a tirade of foul-mouthed abuse and threats to property and person. Dave in 2B had a brick through his window in retaliation for calling the police. Not that the police did much, just issued a warning. Which was ignored.

I've always been the live and let live type, a believer in giving people a chance. But this lot would try the patience of a saint, and I'm definitely not a saint. Being polite and neighbourly didn't work, a warning from the police didn't work. Time for direct action.

My other neighbours and I had co-existed comfortably for years in peace and quiet. It was time to claim it back.

So, last night, after they finally shut up, I slipped out of my room and glided up the stairs. Entering their flat, I made my way to the parents' bedroom. I hovered over their bed and with all the power my long-dead voice could muster, shouted "BOO!"

The bloodcurdling screams that followed rivalled any previous noise they had made. I chased them and their equally obnoxious teenagers all over the flat, blocking their exit whenever they ran for it. I finally left them trembling and sobbing in a corner.

They moved out before breakfast. Peace at last.

Tracy Davidson lives in Warwickshire, England, and writes poetry and flash fiction. Her work has appeared in various publications and anthologies, including: Poet's Market, Mslexia, Atlas Poetica, Modern Haiku, The Binnacle, A Hundred Gourds, Shooter, Journey to Crone, The Great Gatsby Anthology, WAR, In Protest: 150 Poems for Human Rights.

www.twitter.com/tracydavidson27

SENNEN COVE

Amy Howden

The long stretch of Sennen Cove looked different today. The way the white-yellow sand met the sea foam was a thing of breath-taking beauty. The sound of the waves guided my breathing as I looked out at the setting sun. An ombre of colours danced across the cloudless sky.

Today is the perfect day. My brother James stood close to me as we both stared out at the horizon. My young daughters were building sandcastles a few feet away. Their giggles often interrupting an otherwise silent space.

James looked to me after a few moments.

"It's time Helen." I nodded and reached into my bag, retrieving a silver urn from inside.

A sudden bubble of emotion grew inside me, ready to pop. My eyes glistened as my brother took the urn from my hand.

The look on his face was of concern for me yet grief for his own loss, it's hard to see. I remember as a child comforting him when he cried. Now, he's a man and comforting me.

"Are you ready?" My voice cracked, what came out was almost a squeak. My brother gave me a little smile and bobbed his head. He took the lid of the urn and placed it in his pocket. I put my hand inside, grabbing a handful of ashes.

"Mum, I love you." I sobbed. I released the ashes from my hand towards the gentle waves. The ash swirled in the sea breeze like a gymnast's ribbon.

"Rest in peace."

Amy Howden is 35 years old and lives in Widnes, Cheshire. She loves to write about people and their life experiences, good and bad. Her passion for storytelling began as a child. Always an avid reader, Amy's desire to write her own stories came later in life. She's currently working on several short stories and a novel.

www.Instagram.com/amyhowdenwrites

THE WOMAN WHO DROPPED A STITCH

Denny Jace

Hayley knitted cardigans for other people's babies, until Maurice curled his lip. Tonight, she waits until he's sound asleep to knit tiny tank tops for the cade lambs in the farmer's field.

The needles, slick and long, click and slide, as loud as the sky is dark. The carriage clock sits on the mantle, reminding Hayley of her marriage, solid with sharp edges. Its golden hands cut through the precious small hours tutting in syncopation.

Soon the birds will yawn, and daylight will dapple Maurice's cheeks. Hayley folds the tiny tank tops into fluffy piles. She carefully packs them into a carrier bag that she will never give to the farmer for the lambs to never wear. She will stash the bag behind the loose bath panel that Maurice hasn't fixed. Squash it inside, along with the other bags of hope and joy, where the yarn will sweat and rot.

Yesterday, Maurice's brother called. And the day before. He also came the week and the month before that. Bringing her flowers, she could never keep. Soft words and promises of a peaceful life, just out of reach.

Her fanciful musing is quelled by a sudden swell of nausea. Its sour fury racing towards her throat, lubricating her tongue. She breathes it away, counts herself back to calm. In her fingers the cool steel needles twitch. She reaches for her wool, palest yellow. Soon she will knit cardigans for something she will definitely keep.

Denny Jace lives on a farm Shropshire with her husband and their pet lambs, goats, chickens, dogs and cats and has been writing Flash Fiction since June 2019. She has just started work on her first novel.

Her stories have won and listed in Retreat West, Lightbox Originals, Earlyworks Press, Cranked Anvil, Grindstone Literary, Doris Gooderson, Farnham Fringe Festival, Mslexia, Writers Bureau, Strands International, Henshaw, Bridport Flash, HISSAC and NAWG. Published in Ellipsis Zine, Capsule Stories, Bath Flash Fiction, Reflex Fiction, Oxford Flash Fiction, Cabinet of Heed and Writer's Forum magazine.

www.twitter.com/dennyjace

PAIN AND ABLE

Helen Price

His leg hurt but he'd already taken the maximum Paracetamol/codeine mix and the stronger one whose name he couldn't remember beginning with Dic which he always thought funny because that part of his body was about the only place that didn't hurt. Wincing and limping to the bathroom, he managed to shower but arthritic hands made drying and dressing an agony.

'You're lucky,' said the carer when she breezed in for a full ten minutes an hour later. 'Some in my care have real bad pain.'

She swiped clean the centre of the worktop, venturing no further, apparently deterred by the surrounds, maybe no bad thing as she also failed to register the empty whiskey bottles.

'Some can't even get up, Bill,' she continued, her back to him. 'Stuck in bed all day.'

She swung round.

'Fancy a cuppa?'

She reached for the kettle. He nodded. The first shot of the day was beginning to warm his body and numb the nagging nerves. If she smelt it on his breath she didn't say so. But then again, she never got near enough.

'I won't be here next week, Bill, you'll have Kath instead, on hols I am. The Lakes, bitta peace and quiet, leaving the drudge, getting away from it all....'

'Not from yourself, you're not,' said Bill to himself.

'...and maybe walking but definitely relaxing....'

He dashed whiskey from his inner pocket supply into his tea, chuckling in feeling like a movie cowboy.

'Bliss,' he thought, sipping, 'bliss.'

Helen Price lives in Bristol and works as a nurse. She's written three novels but mostly writes short stories. Drawing on a long history in nursing, health and illness are major themes but she's also inspired by environmental and social issues and her early years growing up in Ireland. She's had several short stories published in Scribble magazine and was one of the winners in the 2019 Waterloo Festival Writing Competition (Transforming Being). She was shortlisted in the Percy French Witty Verse competition (2020) and Highly Commended in the Anansi Archive Flash Fiction Competition and published in the Spring Anthology (2022).

A BIT OF A PICKLE

Gillian Scholey

He thrust his boxers out of the shed window and wafted them around. After three days wear they weren't exactly pristine but they were the nearest he had to a white flag. He was used to being in the doghouse, that was part of marriage but he'd never actually been thrown out before. He wedged his garden cane flagstaff into a corner, picked up yet another jar of her pickled onions and slid back down to the floor. Breakfast. Oh, how he yearned for a bacon sandwich.

Everything'd been fine before her works' Xmas do. He'd even lovingly complimented her on her hair, telling her how her curls looked like those of their cockapoo. She'd scowled then and he'd asked if everything was alright. 'Fine' came her answer, so he'd assumed something at work was bothering her. He'd always been intuitive.

Still, it was always better to err on the side of caution so at the party he'd made sure that her boss was in earshot and then he'd told her how bovine she looked in her dress. Sheila had blushed and soon afterwards, at her insistence, they'd left. He'd thought he was on a promise. Women!

*

In the kitchen Sheila clutched her cuppa. It'd been chilly in bed without George to put her feet on. She wondered if he'd been cold. Men! As usual he'd meant well. He always did. Standing, she switched the kettle on and got out George's favourite mug.

Gillian Scholey is from West Cumbria on the fringes of The Lake District. She writes short stories, poetry, flash fiction and plays. Her scripts have been performed by Theatre by the Lake 'Elders',

A SIMPLE HAREM OF SEALS

Julia Ruth Smith

There are fat women at sunset, old women at sunset, red flowers, dead flowers, sailor stripes in blue, green and ochre. They slip into the water without making a sound. They bob like seals, their faces tilted in ecstasy. They tug the hems of their costumes, stroke the lonely whiskers of wisdom.

They bring only tired towels, which they fold in neat squares on the rocks. They measure their distances carefully. This isn't a family affair, not a chattering marketplace, not a festive table.

They tread water with dignity, delighting in cold currents that soothe aching wombs. They open their mouths, moisten their lips, shiver with delight.

They are tired; children and their children like limpets, sharp-toothed men like walrus that sweat and haul themselves begrudgingly through each day, each summer, every single waking hour. Guilt tugs their toes. They shake it off, watch it skitter away; shoals of silver fish.

They've seen many sunsets in their long marriages but they've never heard it stroking waves into small coves, lap-lapping them to sleep, the coolness of evening, still and unhurried.

They're surprised how copper their skin shines, how bright white their nails, how slender their hands gliding through water, pianists, each of them playing their own solos of twilight.

Pink is orange is peach. They smile shyly at each other and breathe. In the final benevolent glory of day they see how truly beautiful they are and christen the first stars in the night sky with their own names.

Julia Ruth Smith is a mother, teacher and writer. She lives by the sea in Italy. Her work has been published by Flashfrog, Reflex Fiction, Skirting Around Magazine and others. She has recently been nominated for Best of the Net by Full House Lit and a Pushcart prize by Seaside Gothic and will appear in the Bath Flash Fiction Anthology this autumn. You can find her on Twitter or at the beach with her dog, Elvis.

www.twitter.com/JuliaRuthSmith1

MESSAGE FROM THE SEA OF TRANQUILITY

Ray Taylor

July 21st, 1969. The big day. As he stood at the top of the ladder, he contemplated the meaning of this awesome achievement. What would the world think?

Still a little jittery, he'd had dreadful butterflies as he clambered into the capsule ready for lift off a few days before. Not as nervous as Otto, though.

"You have your speech ready?" the engineer asked. "The peace message they all want?" Too excited to speak, he just smiled and nodded his reply.

He was calmer now, focused on the next, most dramatic, episode in this outer space odyssey. The first step. He was ready. With a final glance at the ragged horizon (how close it seemed) and the blackness above, he began his descent, step by careful step.

Even as he lowered himself, half skipping, he found it hard to believe he had been chosen for the honour of being the first man. He had lived this moment a thousand times, rehearsing the words he would say as he made the first boot prints on the lunar surface.

Reaching the foot of the ladder, he leapt off and landed with both feet, kicking up a plume of dust into the airless distance above. With a deep breath he lifted his head and spoke into the helmet microphone.

"In 1945 we defeated our enemies and marched on to conquer and pacify the world. Now... we have conquered the Moon! For Führer and Fatherland. Sieg Heil!"

Lest we forget the price of peace.

Raymond Grenville Taylor (b 1959) is a part time government official and author. Ray has been a magazine journalist, a digital media entrepreneur, a company director, and a prison officer. His subjects, themes and genres include history, mystery, sci-fi, love, war, spooky, scary, magic, tragic, witchcraft and wolves. He published his first novel Run with the Pack in 2022 and has published two collections of short stories. Ray lives in Kent, UK, with his wife Sandra and two of their grown-up children. He has a Master of Laws degree (LL.M.) from the Open University.

www.facebook.com/Raymond.G.Taylor.author

Poetry

The poetry category sought entries with a maximum of 12 lines, not including spaces or the title. Many of our entries followed a strict rule of either four or five-line stanzas, but a few challenged this convention.

Poetry is a piece of writing in which the expression of feelings and ideas is given intensity by particular attention to diction (sometimes involving rhyme), rhythm, and imagery.

GIRL IN A CATHEDRAL

Heather Cook

As still as any wooden cross or stone
she sits composed in muted browns and greys,
at peace with both the living and the dead
within this soaring, much-loved space.
Now and then she turns and smoothes a page,
or gazes round, a slight smile on her face.
Perhaps she thinks of martyrs, paupers, kings
who have all shared with her this ancient place.
I'm sure she sings and dances, laughs and weeps,
but now her stillness soothes the ones who sleep.

I'm very much a 'feel it, write it' poet, seeking to capture the emotions and atmosphere of people, places and things. I have always written poetry and can happily lose myself in the process. I belong to a local writers' circle, which has been enormously supportive and a great source of inspiration. Now I'm retired and not so physically active as in previous years, I count myself fortunate to have such a rewarding interest. I haven't yet published a collection, but am thinking of doing so next year. It's a tremendous boost to do well in competitions, but the main thing to me is to enjoy my writing.

https://wokingwriters.wordpress.com/category/heather-cook/

A DROP OF PEACE

Julie Lockwood Austin

On storm filled days you rage and roar and hurl

Yourself towards me. Without a pause, you

Turn and scrape your belly back across the stones.

Long forgotten flotsam gathers at my feet.

On other days, your constant hiss and thrum

Infuses my eyes, my ears, my pores.

That white spray you toss in my direction

Falls like a veil across my face.

From time to time you are still and grey, crinkled

As an old map. Then, I slowly lick

Salted memories from my dry lips and cup

A single drop of liquid peace in my outstretched hands.

After a career largely in education, Julie is currently a part time university student and teacher. Her creative writing tends to focus on issues surrounding class and social and emotional issues linked to being an unpaid carer. She is fortunate enough to live in the South West which provides the backdrop for everything she writes.

FINDING PEACE AT THE BOTTOM OF THE BUCKET

Megan Barber

We are coffee and connection deserving

Its only 10am, already red faced and harassed, cortisol swirling

Under the beautiful illusion that peace will prevail when we reach the park

Scoff, oh what lark

Amidst the tantrums and casualties, we empty buckets of words over each other

Swiftly scoping up handfuls of letters, there is a lot we must cover

The morning stress dribbling down the drain

We laugh at the mess, feel validated and sort of find ourselves again,

A two-way therapy session, multitasking Freuds, less obsessed with sex, more fixated on rest

Later, when I'm home, I wring out the words of the day and I properly hear what you had to say

I soak it up, heart a bit fuller

Me, a bit taller

    The past 7 years of my life have revolved around matrescence, finding my groove with little ones, with work, with life. Motherhood has grown me and forced me to explore my own internal world and connect with my inner child. My role as a play and family therapist means I am often left with extra big feelings to process, not all my own. I needed a way to creatively offload. Spontaneously on my 33rd Birthday this year decided to write a poem about something poignant my Grandma had told me. I had forgotten about the magic of writing. Now I am hooked.

www.instagram.com/meg_a_dele

A NUN'S REFLECTION

Penelope Blackburn

I think about my marriage vows, the deal we made.
I never need to feed him, or clean up after.

No washing the sweat from his work clothes,
no Saturday morning abandonment for DIY or golf.

He never cheated, though he has a thousand other wives.
He was always with me.

I burdened him with my troubles, spoke hard words, railed
and blamed him for making me take the difficult ways.

I trusted him absolutely, even when I questioned,
or doubted him against the harshness of the world.

I let my love grow with my faith – layer by small layer
settling blissfully upon me every reverent day.

Penny Blackburn is from Yorkshire but lives in the North East. Her poetry has featured in a wide range of publications, including Phare, Riggwelter and Poetry Society News. She was recently awarded second place in the Ver poetry competition 2022. She also run a popular spoken word evening in Tynemouth.

www.twitter.com/penbee8

RIVER

Maureen Cullen

when wheat stalks crackle in southern fields
when rapeseed eats up miles of yellow

when roses char to dust on the stem
when the sun bakes our garden ochre

when night sits on my chest like a stone
when my mouth spits ash over the pillow

the Clyde murmurs me to sleep

where sandpipers teeter on pebble and shell
where Canada geese beat—

heartsore to the shore

where an August dusk is a palette of mauves
where an August dawn is a sun-glazed rock.

Maureen lives in Argyll and Bute. In 2015, she was awarded an MA in Creative Writing from Lancaster University. She has stories and poems published in a range of magazines. In 2021, Maureen was shortlisted for the V. S. Pritchett Short Story Prize.

www.twitter.com/maureengcullen

PEACE OFFERING

Christine Griffin

The air was still vibrating
when you offered me cake.
I spurned it.
You put the cake on a flowery plate
I turned to look.
You did your funny face,
put a silver fork in my hand.
I smiled,
took out another fork.
We ate the cake together.

Christine lives in Gloucestershire and enjoys being part of a vibrant literary scene. She loves all forms of writing, particularly poetry and short stories. Christine is widely published both locally and nationally, including in Acumen, Snakeskin, Writing Magazine, Poetry Super Highway and Graffiti Magazine. She has performed her work at the Cheltenham Poetry Festival and the Cheltenham Literature Festival and pre-pandemic she regularly read on local radio.

www.twitter.com/chrissiemg2

300789

Iain McGrath

I linger, alone with you
in your waiting room,
but we cannot embrace.

I listen, alone with you
in your silent room,
but we cannot talk.

Your clock still sounds,
though now it kills time for no one but itself
and I can only hear you in my head,
an echo chamber for grief.

This room is peaceful,
but there can be no peace until we meet again.

Iain McGrath is retired and lives in Nottinghamshire with his wife Claire. Writing is his hobby, and he enjoys trying his hand at a wide variety of genres – pantomimes, plays, poems, short stories, monologues, and song lyrics. 300789 is his first published poem.

UNSPOKEN

Val Ormerod

The silence wraps around you,
a blanket of unspoken words
failing to muffle broken promises.

Lies hover like dragonflies,
waiting to fracture
that fragile peace.

Storm clouds huddle in corners,
plotting their next assault.
The air bristles and crackles.

You watch from a distance,
strangely detached, as if it is not your life
that is about to implode.

Val is a writer and poet from the Forest of Dean, Gloucestershire. She has won the Ware Poets Prize, Magic Oxygen Poetry Prize and Carers UK Writing Competition, and been recognized in the Bridport Prize, Wells Festival of Literature, Plough, and Welsh Poetry Competition. She has an MA in Creative Writing from Bath Spa University and has been published in various anthologies and journals including Stroud Short Stories, Graffiti, Hedgehog Poetry, Ink Tears, Eye Flash Poetry and Reading the Forest. Her memoir In My Father's Memory, about caring for her father, has been adapted into a stage play called My Favourite Dog, performed in the UK and Thailand.

https://twitter.com/Ladybear6

LESSONS

Ana Reisens

Jihad, Qur'ān, Allah: my Arabic vocabulary,
distant sounds of gods and conflict.

She moves closer and traces careful lines on a
white page. Right to left she threads hieroglyphics

across the paper. Left to right she labels their geometric
translations. Together, we transcribe the thick fabric

of sounds. I imitate the movement of her lips and the
curve of the letters with red pen, wondering how to spell

hijab or freedom. Teach me a word, I ask. So she gathers
her ancestry into two sweet syllables and asks me to repeat:

salaam. It's hello, goodbye, an open door
and upturned hand. It means "peace."

Ana Reisens is an emerging poet and writer. She was the recipient of the 2020 Barbara Mandigo Kelly Peace Poetry Award, and you can find her poetry in The Mud Season Review, The Bombay Literary Magazine, and Sixfold, among other places. She lives in Spain and is currently working on her first novel.

https://anareisens.wordpress.com/

WITHHELD VOICE

Sue Spiers

A winter landscape of coat-covered people.
The shock of missile, siege and heavy weapons,
and during sirens, basements dark and silent.

A queue of mothers, children, elders; silent
at the border: a frightened flight of people.
Men stay, turn South and East to face the weapons.

The threat of chemical and nuclear weapons,
not yet deployed, grows soldiers, grim and silent.
The world pleads, 'Stop', to foes and for these people.

When weapons fall silent, these people will speak.

Sue Spiers works with Winchester Poetry Festival, edits the Open University Poetry Society's annual anthology and supports poetry groups Winchester Muse and T'Articulation. Her poems have been published in magazines (14 Magazine, Acumen, Dream Catcher, Dreich, Fenland Poetry Journal, The North, Obsessed With Pipework, Prole, South, and Stand) and on-line (Atrium, The High Window, Ink, Sweat & Tears, The Lake, and London Grip) and in Anthologies (Bloodaxe, Against the Grain, Paper Swans Press)

Sue came 3rd in Battered Moons (2019), commended in Poetry Society Stanza (2020), Binstead (2020, 2021, 2022), Ware (2022), Yeovil (2019) competitions and won Hysteria 4 (2015)

www.twitter.com/spiropoetry

Short Stories

The short story category is for entries of up to 1000 words, not including the title. The short story genre is a staple of writing competitions the world over and many writers will hone their skills in this medium before venturing into the world of longer fiction.

A short story is something that can be read in a single sitting. According to Wikipedia, the written short story emerged from the tradition of oral storytelling in the 17th century.

ET IN ARCADIA EGO

Alexandra Packer

In the trenches Dmytro only ever talked about two things: water and the after.

After he would: kayak the whole length of the Bug, ride the waves in Waimea Bay, swim with the whale sharks in La Paz (which means "peace", he'd explain) and shag at least one member of the national synchronised swimming team.

On that last point we'd laugh: "Dmytro, how are you going to catch one of those mermaids? You can't even swim."

Now here it is at last, the first summer of the after. Maksym and I have taken Dmytro to Arcadia Beach. Odesa is not quite La Paz, but it will have to do.

We're here on a mission, same as everyone else. The treaties are signed, the sea mostly de-mined and the sun is a flaming yellow flower in the pure blue fields of sky, commanding the crowds below to roar from the hymn sheet of happiness. Everyone makes a racket: babies, buskers, common drunks, even mangled freaks like us. Who knew peace would be so noisy?

We find a spot among the tanning throngs, close to the gritty seam between land and sea. Now that we're here, our courage fails us.

Maksym stares out over the water. "Don't think I can do it."

"Let's just sit for a while," I tell him.

We put down a blanket and open up a couple of beers. I shovel in watermelon. Maksym tries to charm some passing girls.

"Spare any sunscreen? Don't want to burn my leg." He points to his prosthetic. The girls giggle.

An older woman comes up to us, round and brown, like an old apple in a swimsuit. She has a child with her, a boy of about 10. She nudges him forward. "Excuse me, but my grandson wants to shake hands with every serviceman on the beach." The boy's eyes are painted buttons, big and blue like the Black Sea. He's clutching a bright yellow backpack.

"That's like starting a collection of the world's ugliest Pokémon," Maksym says. He gives his sharpest salute and puts out his good paw.

The boy doesn't salute back. He shakes our hands solemnly, firmly, stone-faced like an adult. Something bears down on my chest when I look at him, or maybe at any kid these days. I wonder if his ears still ring from the sirens. I look around for his parents.

"How many of us have you found so far, son?" I ask.

The boy doesn't answer. In the din of Arcadia Beach, he's a little island of silence. The blue buttons study Maksym's tattoos: snakes and tridents, poetry and dates.

"Fifteen already," the grandmother fills in proudly. "Seventeen counting you boys."

Maksym reaches into his Spar bag for life and takes out the lacquered wooden box. He sets it firmly in the sand. "Eighteen. This is Dmytro, our medic."

It takes the woman a moment to realise. When she does, she makes a wheezing noise and a sign of the cross. "Jesus and Mary."

The boy stares at the box. He hasn't understood. Why would he? Not many of us around here burn what's left behind. We prefer the cosy confines of familiar earth, warmed by the sunflowers above. But Dmytro, before he bled out, asked for the portable option.

"His poor mother," the woman says, almost tearful. She means the cremation as much as the loss.

"Blessed be her memory," I soothe.

"At least they are together."

Maksym takes a swig of his beer. "Rubbish."

"Rubbish?" The woman draws the boy back by his shoulder, away from us.

"He's not with his mother," Maksym says. "He's right here, on Arcadia Beach. He was a medic, now he's a box. He won the war and now he wants to go for a swim." He taps the box with the foot of his prosthetic. "We're working up to it."

The grandmother has heard enough. "God bless you two," she says and walks off as fast as her flip-flops will let her. The boy stares back at us as he's led away.

"God bless us three," Maksym calls after the woman, then swears. I say nothing. We open another beer and leave Dmytro in the sand to soak up the sun. We stare out at the sea, the quiet part beyond the bobbing spatter of bathers.

Fifteen minutes later, the boy is back. He comes at us full sprint, as if pursued. He skids to a stop with his knees in the sand, checks over his shoulder, shrugs off his backpack and starts to rummage inside.

51

We stare. Even Maksym doesn't know what to say. After a moment, the treasure appears: a large ziploc bag. The boy holds it aloft like a trophy. He shakes it fiercely, dislodging breadcrumbs.

"I'm a good swimmer," he tells us.

We know what he's asking. We ought to say no. It's our job to take the dead swimming. But the child's face is unyielding, and Maksym and I are cowards.

So we huddle in a circle and go to work in silence. The boy holds the bag. Maksym slides in the box. I zip the bag closed and entrust my friend to the safety of the bright yellow backpack.

We get to our feet. The boy loads up and pulls the straps tight. He awaits our command.

"Not too long, okay?" I say. "Come back soon."

Because Maksym and I wouldn't. If we stepped into the water, Dmytro would say: keep swimming. Push away from the noise of these pockmarked shores, speed past the safety buoys, all the way down to the Bosphorus Strait and into the clear cobalt of the Aegean. Swim, he'd say, until you find my mermaids.

But the boy can't hear the dead. He smiles, gives a thumbs up and makes a dash for the sea.

> Alexandra Packer is a Polish writer based in Brighton, UK. Her work has been featured in National Flash Fiction Day's FlashFlood and shortlisted for the Bath Flash Fiction Award. When not working in the tech industry, she bakes and she writes."
>
> https://twitter.com/alexandtheweb

PEACE ON THE NORTHERN LINE

Katherine Birditt

People come looking for me in all sorts of places. Annoyingly, they also tend to frequently mistake me for happiness. However, I am the one who visits every public and private setting imaginable, from concert stages to kitchens- happiness isn't. My personal favourite place to be is the London Underground- there's something about it, all those lost souls yearning for me in the belly of the earth. To feel so deeply desired by all those around you is extremely flattering and, every now and then I must indulge in moments of vanity to keep me sane. My job is after all dreadfully disheartening most of the time.

Today I'm on the Northern line, my favourite of all the lines. At this moment it is Margret who's searching for me. I have met her before in other places at other times. She's on her way to Highgate, which has been her home for almost all of the seventy-six years she's hard on earth. This fact seems to simultaneously exude a sense of great fortune and feeling of despair. Her husband Matthew sits next to her. I don't recognise him so he must be one of the rare, lucky ones who has never once had to worry about looking around for me in libraries and sunsets.

As Margret sits there in the stale, sutured silence of the carriage I take her on a slight detour, down the branch of memory to a time when she was twenty-one. I have a good partnership with memory, we work well together. Margret's eyes take on a faraway look and I know she's seeing that old tube interior of the Northern line clearly. Sandra's laugh from the seat to her right washes over her again. I take her back to Friday, that special Friday where her and Sandra's journey ended amongst the lights of Leicester square. Their families had been sitting around tables at home having Friday night dinner as they had always done. However, Sandra and Margret were now free from the grand ritual of it all by virtue of their age. Their mothers were no longer able to force them to follow customs and say prayers. I had inevitably crept up on them all those years ago, in a way that was, looking back, cruel and unfair because it had left Margret searching for me for the rest of her life in vain. I'm by no means perfect unfortunately.

Margret holds me, reliving the sense of peace that I reserve for being twenty-one in London, a little drunk off cheap corner store wine and with multiple somewheres still left to go. This was the night that Sandra would later kiss her for the very first time, right by the station entrance. It was a quivering storm of desire that had been brewing for far too long and so I was there too beneath the tube roundel moon to drench them in my presence. It was a clumsy, greedy kiss, hidden in the shadows and fuelled by a confidence that the white wine had loaned them for the night. Margret feels the entire thing all over again- surprised I have returned to her after all this time. I feel her bask in me as she recalls the wet warmth of Sandra's mouth and the complimentary curve of hardened breasts against her own with an intimacy that makes me blush.

Matthew says something just then, dragging her away from me back to reality. She looks around for me desperately, disappointed and lost like a tourist in the rain. He speaks words that only she is meant to hear. She smiles and replies and takes his hand, all the while begging me to come back to her. For a moment I wish I could, but that goes against both my policies and principles. Accordingly, I move down the carriage, leaving her thinking sadly how one learns to live with a lot and to live without even more.

~

There's a man in the same carriage, a little further down from Margret and Matthew who I visit next. If you were to guess his name, you'd go with something like Gary or Todd. However, I know he is in fact Chris. I also know he can't bring himself to cry right now having grown up in the north of England where men do not cry openly and instead search for me in pub bathrooms. Chris, up until that morning had never met death, at least not properly. The memory of his dead father in the hospital is painfully fresh and, at only one hour old, has barely even become a proper memory yet. I approach Chris, taking him away from the hospital with its constant beep of machines and stench of disinfectant-drenched death. There's not much time left though. I have to get off at Camden. I must be quick with Chris and so I pull out my oldest trick, opening his eyes to the present, this very moment in the tube.

At first Chris is shocked and hesitant when I touch him, a part of him unsure as to whether he should willingly accept peace at this time. However, I am far too good at my job and have been doing it for much too long for him to succeed in resisting me. I ground him in the gentle rocking of the tube, the sound it makes on the tracks, the way the world outside is shrunk to a softened blur. He surrenders, melting into me and I stay with him until we reach the next stop.

I look back at Margret and Chris as the tube leaves Camden. Their faces are shadowy blurs and will remain that way until we find each other again.

I'm a biomedical science student, aspiring neurologist and somewhat surprisingly a writer in my spare time. Growing up in Harare, Zimbabwe my love for stories was instilled within me from a young age. Today this passion for writing has travelled with me to London where it has expanded and diversified, such that I now write broadly, across science art and creative fiction. Writing is a way for me to explore concepts and ideas that span not only disciplines but also emotional landscapes.

FLIGHTS OF FANCY

Yvonne Clark

It was Saturday, and I was in Bali.

Clouds fanned out against the skies like the wings of collared doves. The tide left in its wake a tracery of effervescent foam, and gamelan music lulled me into a cushion of dreams, a pillow of peace. Granny would love it here. I stored away the sights and sounds in my mind to recount to my grandmother later.

'Shoes off! Your buckles will scratch the leather seats.'

My father's gruff smoker's voice startled me out of my reverie.

Long before seat belts were compulsory, I would lie across the back seat of the Ford Cortina, gazing out of the windows, tracking the trail of neon street lights, allowing myself to be sucked into a parallel universe away from my parents in the car, arguing, always arguing.

I liked Sundays best. On Sundays Mum didn't visit Granny so there were no arguments. 'She's your Mum, she doesn't want to see me,' Mum would say to my father. I still sat in the back seat, though, alone with my dreams.

Last Sunday I was in Japan, 'Land of the Rising Sun'. A solitary stork, white as a geisha girl's face, was illuminated against the shadow of Mount Fuji. And was that steam rising from the hot springs where monkeys bathed? I gazed at the snow-capped mountains, their valleys glowing with a cocktail of turquoise, pink and gold as they drank in the early morning light. When I told Granny, her eyes lit up with a mixture of sunshine and rain.

Mum and Dad drank too much. Not cocktails. He drank beer, lots of it, I could smell it on his breath when he kissed me. Did Granny notice, I wondered? If so, she didn't say. Granny was saying less and less these days. But she liked to listen, especially to the tales of my fictitious travels.

Mum drank wine. She started at lunchtime and continued until News at Ten. Sometimes longer.

When my parents argued, they didn't even notice what time I went to bed. This had some good points: they didn't check how late I was playing computer games or whether I had brushed my teeth properly. But sometimes the shouting crescendoed and I would bury myself deep into my duvet, hands pressed against my ears. If it stopped me sleeping, I would pull back the curtains and gaze at the sky, its inky blue canvas peppered with silver sequins of stars, and think about the next country I would visit.

Australia, perhaps. Mum was always going on about wanting to live there. Better weather, better jobs, a better life all round, she said, but Dad said it was too far, and what about Granny? Mum always said that if she hadn't met Dad, she would be living there by now. She told me she may still go, but that it was our secret.

There were plenty of other choices. Italy, with its Vatican city, Verdi operas and vineyards? The flamenco music, festivals and fabulous beaches of Spain? Or the fashion and culinary sophistication of France? In the end I decided to combine all three. Who knew how much time Granny had left. Poor Granny, she always wanted to travel and now she couldn't. I tried to bring every country to life for her.

At bedtimes I read National Geographic while my parents' belligerent banter drifted up the stairs. I devoured the photographs like a starving dog; inhaled the descriptions like an addict, knowing that my mind could transform the monochromatic text into a kaleidoscope of colour.

The following Saturday was blisteringly hot. I lay in the back of the car as usual, the skin of my legs sticking to the PVC upholstery, stinging me every time I peeled them into a different position. I Rorschached the clouds into the images I had been reading about. Vapour trails of airplanes criss-crossing the sky became banners announcing the feast day parade of a Spanish saint, while clouds erupted into the domes of the Doges Palace and Saint Peter's Basilica. All the time the scene was changing, changing, morphing into images captured in my mind.

Did I have to die before I could reach this place? I knew my grandfather was there, like all the other dead people. Mum told me every star was a person who had died. But how did you know which star was which person, there were so many? When Granny died, would she be able to find Grandad? Maybe I would ask my father tomorrow when Mum wasn't in the car. Dad could navigate by the stars — he was a naval officer. He would have the answers.

But that Sunday was to be a different sort of day. Granny's health took a turn for the worse overnight, so all of us went to the nursing home. The rash of rain on the car windows merged and trickled down the windscreen like the tears which fell down my father's face, and the mood in the car was solemn and silent. No arguments that day. I was sad because I had been keeping my best destination for Granny until last: The United Kingdom. There was no need to look up into the sky. Mountains and lakes, quaint coastal villages, rich rural landscapes and cities bursting with historical and architectural gems. We had it all.

'We're in the best country, Granny,' I would say when I saw her.

As my parents spoke to the care home manager I tried not to listen, but caught her last words, '... at peace.'

My parents held each other tightly for a few moments, then clasped hands as we went into Granny's room. Seeing them like that made me happy, even though they were sad. And when I looked at Granny's face, she looked happy, too. She would never need me to take her on imaginary journeys any more.

She had gone on a journey of her own, in search of Grandad's star.

After working for many years in editorial publishing, Yvonne became a teacher of academic EFL in the UK and abroad. Her foray into flash fiction and short story writing coincided with the outbreak of the Covid pandemic in 2019, and her work has had success with a number of publishers.

She lives in Chichester in West Sussex, where the beautiful South Downs and coastal landscapes provide an inspirational environment for a writer to live in. She is a passionate supporter of animal welfare and environmental issues.

AT THE END OF THE DAY

Heather Haigh

Peace is the slip-snick of bamboo needles, and the barely perceptible rasp of yarn over loose-fitting skin. The yarn is called Beaches; it's variegated, so I can lose myself in the rhythm of the work as the colours reveal themselves—slowly, patiently, as they will: Champagne pink, like the sunset over Filey that heralded time for our fish supper. Blue-grey—like cool water that kissed tired feet as we strolled along the margin between sand and sea, savouring the caress of soft foam on hot skin. Blushing white like streaks of candyfloss pulled across a cerulean sky, beckoning the Skua to soar.

Busy hands make restful minds.

The age spots on the back of my hands resemble the shadows on the swollen face of a harvest moon. Do you recall those nights: the gentle lap of lake against shoreline, the lonely call of a tawny owl reaching into the darkness, the brush of a scarce umber moth against papery beech leaves?

I can almost hear the rustle of newspaper, the tap of a thoughtful pen. My breath catches as I wait for your enquiring cough.

I would shake my head. 'Thirty-one, thirty-two, thirty-three ... '

You'd wait patiently for the end of the row, then: 'Pregnant or egg-bearing, six letters, last one D?'

'Gravid.'

Gravid—like the hens that wandered around your sister's garden, determined to tear the petals from every last pansy.

'No gratitude for their rescuer.' You'd shake your head and tut.

The hens would scratch at the sandy earth, self-satisfied chortle-clucks rising into the afternoon haze, while we sipped glass-frosting lemonade and shared bread-from-the-oven-warm anecdotes. Tales of our youth when we scrambled over dry-stone walls to scrump crab apples, or sat on sun-baked earth rolling click-clack marbles into holes burrowed out by short fat fingers. Memories of summers tossing bread to gluttonous ducks and autumns hurling sticks into recalcitrant horse chestnuts. We recalled winters sledging down a snow-covered Canon-ball Hill. Days spent well, before we trudged home wrapped in dusk's misty cloak and companionable fatigue.

Where once we hoarded the days of youth, now I treasure the golden hours of our twilight. Memories of memories, ghosts of joy.

I can still hear your footsteps crunching solemnly over hymn-sanctified gravel. I can taste the whisper of fragrance from the Dianthus you clutched.

'Rest in peace, Sister,' you murmured.

Gravid—like my swollen belly, before it burst a pair of squalling people into our life. To hold, to fret over, to wave into the world. Double-trouble, toil and tussle, matching grins and secret gossip. Head-to-head they shared plans, mischief, and nits. At the end of day, I would patch torn dungarees, while you mended a wheel-less cart. I would hunt for elusive gym shoes, while you pumped up bicycle tyres. I would towel-hug squirming splash-monsters, while you washed the dishes. Then the clock would briefly slow its ticking for story time, as we all wound down, ready for that sigh when tiny heads are full of dreams and we turned at last to our time.

A girl, who listened wide-eyed to stories of steam trains and woodland creatures, now sends an occasional letter. The latest explained how the elephants' food must be hidden around their enclosure to encourage them to roam. The girl needed no prodding.

'Dad would love to know that.'

'He would.'

A boy, who nestled close as tales of merfolk and magical islands swam around him, phoned at the weekend to tell of his day recording the colour changes of the cephalopods in his care.

'Dad would have loved to see that.'

You would.

Then.

It's quiet.

Again.

Pregnant—like the silence that stretches when I pause at the end of a row. Silence that stretches into the night when I lay my knitting aside. Like the silence before the words spoken above you. And the silence after.

There's no peace for me in silence. Peace is a whoosh, a flutter, and a whoop on a kite-flying day, a splash, a ripple and a giggle on a poohsticks day, the patter of footsteps and muted sniggers on a lazy, hazy, maze day.

Peace is those moments worked for. Fleeting moments stolen between the end of a full-to-the-brim, blink-and-you-miss-it day and the eternity of an empty night. Moments cherished, as I wait for another time, another place. Until then, rest my love.

Rest.

Heather is a disabled, working-class writer, from Yorkshire. She found the joy of writing late in life. Her words have been published by: Reflex press, Anansi Archives, Black Moon Magazine and others. She likes to make and wear silly hats.

haigh19c.wixsite.com/heatherbooknook

REST IN PEACE

Valerie Hoare

The old lanes haven't changed much, the birds are still arguing in the hedges, fighting over food. You'd think there was a war on. Well, there was when I left. I marched away in full kit, rifle and bayonet, I've only got a suitcase to carry now. And this cheap suit to wear. It's quite warm, the sky's still bright blue, and the clouds pearly white. At least I'm home before winter.

Back in Germany, I tried not to think of home, it felt like I was pushing my luck. Just get through another day, Joe, that's what I told myself. All around me men were falling like skittles, I just wanted to survive.

Course, I had good reason to come home. Some of them, like Charlie Dawes, they sort of gave up. He was my mate, was Charlie, we'd been together from the start. Shared a few laughs and a smoke when we had one, and a few foxholes, too. But he lost his way once he heard about the bomb. Lost everything else that day, his wife and his mother, and his pretty little girl.

It never seemed such a long walk from the station before, but I was younger then, I used to run it. I was top of the class in sprinting, not much good in lessons but full of energy outside. That was before I started smoking, though.

Then when I finished school I got a job at the timber mill with Mr Burton. I should be able to see the yard over the hedge here. Now, either I've shrunk or that hedge has got taller, I can't even reach the top. The troop trucks coming through must've pushed the bank back off the road, it leans away from me. There's a gap where the cows have rubbed at it, I can see through. Yes, there's the shed and if I listen I can just hear the saws humming.

I met Susan on a day out in Southsea. I was with the lads from the yard, she was with the girls from the leather factory. Easter '39, it was, before the madness began. It was her smile I noticed first, the way it made her eyes crinkle, not just her mouth. We hit it off

straight away.

We started courting and never looked back. It was quite a trip to visit her at the weekend, all the way over in Southampton, but we kept it going for a year. Then her Dad agreed to us getting married, just before I was called up. We had just a week or two together so we started decorating our little flat. She liked yellow for the walls, I wanted blue so we compromised on green. I made her a wooden coffee table too.

I've treasured all the letters she sent me while I was away. They kept me going when times were rough. I've read them to bits in so many places, in the training camp, then in Europe before they sent me to North Africa. I got wounded there, not bad enough to get me home, though. Just local leave.

There was some proper leave later, after we'd finished our bit, but I had to go back after two weeks. There wasn't much time to get used to being home, barely enough to agree with Susan on names for our boy, Peter. He was just a baby then, I haven't seen him since. I've never met our little girl, Anne, she was born while I was in Italy. Susan sent pictures of them with her letters. I wonder what they'll think of me.

They won't know me, perhaps Susan won't either. I've changed a lot, got a bit knocked about one way and another. There's beauty out there but you can't forget what you've seen, hellish places you've been, grim things you've had to do. None of us are the same. You can't explain it to people who weren't there, not even family.

I couldn't tell them I was coming, I wasn't sure when I'd get here. With all the paperwork and regulations I had to wait my turn. I tried reading some poems, looking for peace. Some I could understand, others left me cold.

I should see the houses soon, round the next bend. I'm glad they moved out here to the country with my Ma. Lord knows what might've happened if they'd stayed in the City. They had it bad down there, with the bombs.

We'll have to start again, I suppose, with our own place, I don't know how we'll

manage. Mr B said he'd keep my job for me but no-one expected it would take so long

to stop the Nazis. I can't believe I've been away four years. One minute I think I'm just a lad then I look in my shaving mirror and see what I've become. An old man of twenty five, grey hairs, wrinkles, the lot.

I've got just one cigarette left, I'll stop for a smoke. I've promised myself I won't buy any more once I get home, but I'm nervous now, sweating. What if Susan doesn't want me, maybe she's got someone else? It's a big moment, just turning up like this. Perhaps I should've told her I was on my way.

But I'll never know unless I face her. After all I've faced these past years, the horrors I've seen, I have to take this last step. I throw down my smoke and tread it out.

Old Mrs Plumb in the corner house spots me first, she never did miss much. She peers at me and her hands go to her mouth. She's out the gate and across the street, straight up to Ma's door before you can say boo. No dithering now, I quicken my pace.

Sue comes out the gate, waving. Her smile looks just the same, her dark hair still shines in the sun. I drop my case and run to her.

Ever since getting a manual typewriter for Christmas at eleven years old, Valerie has written short fiction. Around retail work and then family commitments, there have been some successes in short story competitions over the years, though not as many as she would've liked. Often regretting her lack of further education, she always hoped to return as a mature student but life got in the way. Now retired, she still feels there is more to come. Searching for wider spaces, she has completed two novels that are still looking for homes. Valerie has two grown children and four grandchildren.

IN PURSUIT OF PEACE

Taria Kavillion

People sometimes ask me why I work in a morgue. I tell them that, being one of seven siblings, I may have subconsciously sought a job with plenty of peace and quiet, where the customers never complain or give you stress. Never, that is, until tonight.

It wasn't like one of those cheesy scenes where the cadaver sits bolt upright and there's an 'B' movie scream from the helpless heroine that even my deaf Gramma could hear. It just sounded like somebody on the phone in another room. Or so I thought. Living in a small town and working in a very small hospital, you soon get to know most people's voices, but I didn't recognise this one. Eventually it dawned on me - it was a radio being switched on and off, over and over. Curiosity and annoyance soon got the better of me, and I went to track it down.

When I found myself at the morgue lockers, I figured either someone was playing a prank on me, or it was what the county Sheriff liked to call an 'stangow' - a Stag Night Gone Wrong.

A couple of deep breaths and a warm coat later, I heaved the drawer open. The body bag was wriggling about like a big, black caterpillar, but silently save for the odd bursts of radio adverts and twangy riffs of crackly country music.

I can honestly say I've seen 'stangow' bodies - live ones and dead ones - in all kinds of get-ups. Tutus, nappies and nothing more than good ol' fresh air, but this was different again – one vivid, spandex bodysuit, hefty platform boots and some kind of motorcycle helmet. What I couldn't see, in either of their huge gloved hands, was a radio. Gloves, though, thankfully – at least there'd be no frostbite to be sued over.

Removing the helmet revealed young-ish, vaguely foreign-looking features and a bald head. I might even have given him a second look, if a) we were in a bar rather than a morgue, and b) he didn't look like he was trying to audition for the Village People. I decided he was likely deaf too, because was waving his hands around like a conductor with a bladder weakness. Thankfully, my Gramma taught me to sign. She used to say two deaf people from different countries are better equipped to communicate than two hearing people. (This from the women who smilingly turned off her hearing aid at the nightly Waltons-style dinner table fiasco!) So, as best I can remember, the 'conversation', such as it was, went something like this;

'It's ok, you're safe... Do you know where you are?'

'No! Where is this?'

'You're in a hospital. Do you know what happened? Are you hurt?'

His oversized hands patted his torso and legs.

'I am ok. I fell out of my (something) and I woke here! My group will come back for me.'

I admired the guy's optimism.

'Our Sheriff must have thought you were dead. Or did your friends - your 'group' – bring you here? Are you a bridegroom?'

No response. This had long night written all over it.

'Can I call someone for you?'

At this point he started to emulate a ninja fighting off a swarm of bees, and held up my arms.

"I'm sorry, fella, but I have two tenths of no clue what you're trying to say." He gave a grunt and pointed to the door, and eventually I followed him outside.

Now, nights in New Mexico can get pretty darn cold, and this guy was in nothing much more than a trapeze artist outfit, but I swear he was warmer than the patio heaters at Blanche's Diner. He was squinting through the swirls of desert dust dancing in the midnight breeze. Then, tilting his bald head like an eagle on a telegraph pole, he lifted his arm and pointed at the distant mountain range.

'I am from there... Far away... I receive an invitation. I read about this place – my group come to observe wars... We learn, go home, stop our wars.'

'Oh, not a wedding guest, then? You're a student? ... a journalist?'

More blank looks. The guy scanned the ground before picking up a long stick. My feet acted faster than my brain and took a few paces back. To my relief, he started drawing in the sandy dirt. A map, maybe? A flag? I held my arms wide and shrugged.

Another grunt. He was pointing at the scrawls, then again at the horizon, but I couldn't see squat.

His shoulders slumped, and he looked down at me with those big black eyes. I suddenly got the feeling that he was younger than he looked.

'Do you know anyone here?'

'No – my group come back soon – they will take me home'

At that, his head drooped still further, and I didn't need any language to tell he wasn't enthused by the idea.

'Are you ... scared to go back?'

'No, but I don't want to go – home is very crowded and noisy.'

'Oh, I hear you, buddy, I do. In my home, I'm one of seven siblings!' I held up seven fingers and waggled them for emphasis.

There was an odd, scoffing noise – was he laughing, belching or choking? But what happened next nearly made me choke. I had to be hallucinating! He was removing his gloves and – as I watched – his big 'hands' unfurled into a mass of tendrils – like fat spaghetti waving out of his sleeves. Pleeease let this be where I wake up at my desk! But it was all horribly real - there was Spandex Goliath, nonchalantly holding up literally dozens of 'fingers', whilst beyond him, low in the desert sky, a ring of lights raced toward us.

As I started to lose grip on consciousness and the ground suddenly seemed much closer, I could see him signing.

'I am one of seventy siblings... I just wanted a job with some peace and quiet!'

Taria Karillion grew up in a tiny cottage in the grounds of a Welsh castle, and is supposedly descended from an infamous pirate (a discovery that made her fencing coach laugh out loud). Her historical background drew her to the fantasy genre like a blob of gravy to a white shirt. That changed, however, after an accident with a flight of stairs, 'The Hitch-hiker's Guide to the Galaxy' and a nasty attack of gravity, all of which resulted in a partial defection to science-fiction fandom. An adolescence surrounded by far more books than is probably healthy for one person, and a degree in Literature only made things worse.

Her work has been likened by judges and editors to Douglas Adams and Neil Gaiman, and her stories (nearly forty to date) have appeared in a Hagrid-sized handful of anthologies, and have won enough awards to half-fill his other hand. Despite this, she has no need as yet for larger millinery.

For a flavour of some of her other work, take a look at her website. Maybe on one of those dull, rainy Sundays when you're trying to keep your mind off that one pigeon that's resolutely eyeing up your newly washed car.

jrt301.wixsite.com/tariakarillion

A PEACE OF CHOCOLATE

Marie Keiding

"Oh, it's the fat one."

The words etch little chinks in Jenny's carefully constructed armour.

She doesn't want to give the crowing figure in the bed the satisfaction of seeing the words hit their mark, so she crosses the linoleum floor at a brisk pace. With each step, Jenny's 10 o'clock chocolate bar makes comforting little thumps against her thigh.

The coarse fabric of the curtains scratches against her fingers when she flings them open. Another rainy morning. The grey light matches the furniture in the white walled room. A visiting interior designer once referred to the decorating style as institutional chic. Doesn't matter. No amount of designer ingenuity would make a difference to the underlying odour of concentrated urine and disinfectant.

"Are you trying to blind me?" The hissing between laboured breaths channels more snake than human.

Jenny checks to make sure her armour is intact before she turns around and flashes Mrs. George a professional smile.

"You rang, Mrs. George?"

A twig of an arm waves like a reed in the wind. Before Mrs. George can follow up the movement with some ridiculous demand, a coughing fit overtakes the fragile body. The rattling of fluid in the lungs makes Jenny think of her decrepit coffeemaker at home.

With each cough Mrs. George works harder to mobilize her dwindling strength. The intervals get longer and longer … and longer until finally the coughing stops.

Spent, Mrs. George leans back in the light blue bedding. She doesn't even object when Jenny wipes pink froth from her wrinkled mouth with a damp cloth.

As Jenny rinses the cloth, she keeps an eye on her patient's chest. It has yet to move after the coughing fit. Jenny's training kicks in and her attention flickers from chest to wall clock and back again. A deep wrinkle pulls at the skin between her eyebrows.

Ten seconds, twenty seconds. Jenny locates the red emergency buzzer near the door. Come on, old bird!

A slight rise of the duvet makes Jenny call off her mental emergency readiness. Watery eyes peek out under half closed lids.

The voice from the bed is hoarse and low.

"Don't look so pleased, I'm not dead yet."

Jenny folds her arms on her massive bosom. She bites down lightly on her tongue.

"Why did you ring the buzzer before, Mrs. George?"

"Remembers like an elephant, that one."

Months ago, Jenny would have given Mrs. George the benefit of the doubt. Experience and the quick glance in Jenny's direction assures her that the snide remark was meant to be heard.

Too bad the only way out of this job is to win the lottery.

Mrs. George has regained a little strength. She reaches out and gets hold of a shiny red and white handbag on the messy bedside table. With determination the bedridden madam pours the contents on the duvet; mints, used bus tickets and all.

After a minute, a small dry hand triumphantly holds up a lightly crinkled 4 x 6-inch picture. Mrs. George waves it in Jenny's direction.

The picture shows an overweight woman in a mint green tracksuit. She sports a frizzy perm and enormous glasses. She's smiling at the camera and showing a big bar of chocolate to the photographer.

Jenny pulls her armour close around her and hands the picture back to Mrs. George.

The airy voice is almost inaudible. "It's me."

Jenny's eyebrows betray her. They shoot up until they are not even visible under her hairline.

"This is you?" she asks, eyes wide.

"That," the flabby excess skin on her upper arm bounces back and forth as she waves the picture around, "was the happiest …"

A wheezing intake of breath interrupts the sentence.

Mrs. George pauses to pick through the debris of the content of the handbag. She locates a grubby inhaler, shakes it, and inhales its content with expertise. She exhales in slow motion.

"The happiest days of my life."

It's more the gesture that follows than the words themselves that makes Jenny think of an olive branch. A dry, wrinkled, backhanded specimen, but an olive branch none the less.

Mrs. George moves a little sideways under the duvet and pats her hand lightly on the edge of the bed.

Jenny wants to reach out and take the olive branch, but her armour tells her no. A leopard doesn't change its spots, a snake doesn't … well, something.

In the bed Mrs. George is nibbling on her lower lip. She's staring at a smudge on the duvet. Jenny's still on the fence when her warm palm is cooled by a wrinkled touch.

A deep sigh escapes from somewhere inside her.

The bed creaks as Jenny leans one buttock on the edge of it. She tilts her head up a bit, daring the grey-haired menace to spit her venom.

A sly smile forms on the craggy landscape. Blue eyes twinkle with mischief as they flicker from Jenny's eyes to the square outline in her pocket and back again.

Jenny's shoulders relax as the armour inside of her uncoils. The laugh that escapes her lips makes the bed bounce.

The 10 o'clock chocolate bar is a bit warm from the contact with her thigh, but it breaks easily into two equal parts. She hands one half to Mrs. George.

Mrs. George puts the chocolate to her nose and inhales. Just from witnessing the gesture, the scent of cacao, sugar, and almonds flood Jenny's nostrils. She takes a bite, and watch the old woman follow her lead.

Marie grew up in a yellow house in Vejle, Denmark. As a child she desperately wanted to be one of Enid Blyton's "The Famous Five", but ended up pursuing a steadier career as a nurse. In her experience most patients are a lot nicer than Mrs. George. Marie is currently working on her first crime novel and more short stories.

www.facebook.com/mk2stories

WHO ARE THE WITCHES

Denarii Peters

We came for the sake of peace. We came for our children. We brought their pictures, their small, outgrown booties and the occasional babygrow. We took our soft reminders of those we loved and we pinned them or tied them to the hard, stark metal wires of the fence that was so much taller than we were.

Beyond that fence were the soldiers. We brought them sweets but they had mouths full of complaints. They had been ordered to fell English oaks and elms in order to give American guns a clearer shot at British women. One said he was willing to place his own body between the guns and us. He said he had never enlisted for this.

There were eight of us. We had travelled in our minibus from Yorkshire singing, "We shall not be moved!" We brought our tents, our cook stoves, our expensive fleece lined sleeping bags, our picnic of chicken and salad. We were going to walk the perimeter, all six miles of it. We would run our fingers over the wire. We would visit the Gate, the earliest one to be founded, yellow like the sun on the badges, then walk all the way to the Green Gate, where no men were allowed. We brought gifts for the "wimmin", cigarettes, coffee, soap, vegetables, warm blankets... We had been told they slept in "benders". We knew the word but the reality of the clear plastic tunnels on the ground, some patched where the police had ripped them open time and again, was more than we had been prepared for, more than we had foreseen in our comfortable middle class plans.

We were half way round when the van pulled up on the verge a little way ahead of us. A dozen unkempt, dirty, half dressed women tumbled out with a photographer.

"Lots of hugs and kisses, girls!" He shot them over and over playing at being lesbians then they clambered back into the van and vanished into the distance.

"The Sun does that every few days. Got to keep up the headlines, haven't they?" explained one weary squaddie looking on with bored disinterest.

On we went past a small party of police. "Don't know why you lasses keep coming. This has nothing to do with you."

We replied in chorus, "We are here for peace! We are here for our children!"

Green Gate and a friendly welcome. We were part of the sisterhood and - did we know? - two more women had been arrested that morning. They had wriggled through a hole in the fence and danced on top of a silo before the soldiers got to them. They'd be martyrs now.

We sat and we sang. I learned the chorus of Anne Hill's song, "Who Are the Witches?" so well I have never forgotten them. Yes, we saw ourselves as the wise young women of the day.

Night and it was cold, snuggled down in our warm sleeping bags. Then, just after midnight, the police roused us. Headlights on the tents, we had to get out so they could search.

"What for?" we demanded.

They had no answers, did not want to talk to us. They wrote down the number of the minibus, agreed we had a right to camp on the common land but still said we should not be there. Then everything was thrown out of the tents onto the muddy, wet ground.

Sleeping again. Two o'clock, more police, same search... and again, just after four.

Tired in the morning but at least our tents were intact. Some of the benders had been slashed while the women inside tried to sleep.

Back to Yorkshire, still singing.

A few weeks later in December 1983 and even the Sun was forced to admit there were more than fifty thousand of us this time. Coach after coach. I had never seen so many coaches or so many women in one place. Again the pictures on the fence and this time hands joined in a six mile ring, so many of us it was five deep in places. Where I was there were so many pressing against the fence it began to buckle and sway. I was at the front, my hands grasping the wires, my feet slipping in the mud. I was terrified. It was a vertical sea heaving with upright waves, forward, back, forward, back.

The elation evaporated, sheer terror replaced it. I believed utterly in the cause. We were right to care but - oh! - I did not want to be crushed into the churned up mud of Greenham Common. Forward, back, forward, back, the fence shifting, tearing at its roots.

Somehow I was no longer clinging on. The fence had fallen forward and some women raced across the tangled wire, dodging the soldiers beyond, singing their songs of peace. I was not one of them. I did not have the speed... or the courage. I did not dance on a silo that day but I like to think I was part of the music.

Denarii was born in the north-west of England. She now lives with her husband in Norfolk, where the weather is much drier. She is often found reading or spying on a small herd of muntjac deer which have taken over the gardens outside her flat. A former primary school teacher, she spends her days writing stories of all kinds, primarily in the young adult fantasy genre, and drinking a lot of coffee. In recent months she has or is soon to have four other short stories published in various anthologies.

AN ABSTRACT PEACE

Owen Wall

The button is a lie.

I know a button that has killed more people than The Black Death, than the Spanish Flu, than any recent crisis. It is small and it is grey, and it is insultingly ordinary in its appearance. It should be the size of my head. It should be sunburn-red and the most conspicuous, most extraordinary button the world has ever seen. But it's not, and therefore the button is a lie.

When I dream of it, it is void-black, rotting – shaped like an apple core – but the body of the apple is pure light, and from it spreads tendrils that reach and reach and reach and when they touch, they heal. I've always had abstract dreams. An abandoned lollipop on a museum floor. A dancing hippopotamus riddled with bullet holes. My dad – a shrink – always told me to read into them, break them down and find their meaning. Until the button, I'd thought this a stupid activity. Dreams were dreams. There was no hippopotamus in my life that needed shooting up. But the button... it taught me otherwise. My dreams did mean something. And the dreams saved me... and doomed a million more.

I sat in the clouds, moving among them. The sky was dark, a navy blue. Night was a fitting time for death – they were ready for bed, why not put them in it? My metal tomb rattled around me, and I found the familiar thoughts rising.

I saw the city now. Could see its lights, its high-rise buildings, its unique architecture. I imagined I could see them down there. I always see them as termites. The buildings that would crush them, mounds of dirt. The abstract nature of my dreams had bled into my waking thoughts of recent years. A defence. The termites below were swarming a humungous wire, digging their serrated mandibles into it, gripping and tearing away strips with frenzy. That wire reached for miles – in-fact it circled the entire Earth, before burrowing down and down, into the heart of the world itself. There were many wires like this. And many termite nests. And if I didn't push my button, if I didn't clear the infestation, the heart could not beat…

I am a saviour. The world is gripped in the worst disease it's ever given birth to. War. But this war is a special one. It is a war that must be fought, for victory means the decimation of the thing itself. To win the war would mean Peace, forever. And so, when I push my button – my rotten, yet healing, apple core – I am giving Peace. I am giving Peace… Peace… Peace, I repeat the word a thousand times in my head as I approach. Soon I'm saying it aloud.

"Peace. Peace. Peace," like a mantra of mine. In my mind, Peace is a plated meal. It is a meal of countless components – broccoli, chicken, potatoes, carrots – and each of these foods are spread across the plate in snaking lines – green or white or brown – and they intersect, but when they do, they do not overlap, but pass by tidily. No bean juice intrudes on the shells of the muscles.

The moment was near for the button to be pushed, and so I forced this plate into my mind. I saw it in the clouds. In the control panel. Behind my eyelids. If it threatened to slip, I would force it back, and repeat, repeat, repeat, that word that I was doing this for. But sometimes… there was the odd slip.

I found myself with trembling hands. Breathing wasn't as effective as usual. My cockpit seemed half the size. I'm about to kill again. I wouldn't see them die. I wouldn't hear them scream or see the horror in their eyes as their world was torn in two. I wouldn't know how they felt as their families and neighbours were scorched, immortalised as shadows upon the pavement. But my finger would deliver it to them. I pictured the plate. "The war to end all wars," they told me. The politicians. The army leaders, the allies. I wondered if the other side said it to their bombers too. "Obliterate this city, and we will have peace!" "Slaughter these innocents, and war will be no more!" "Kill for us. Kill for us and never stop killing for us, because at the end, upon a pile of corpses and ash, there will be peace!"

Peace... It was that pleasant dream that you couldn't quite see to the end, for something would wake you. Something would shatter its illusion – incinerate its inhabitants and topple its buildings. Next time, you'd think. Next time I'll see the dream to the end. Next time I won't have to wake up, won't have to be disturbed... we've been saying this for fourteen years now. I've been dropping my dream-breakers for nine.

I have murdered millions, but that is ok. It's ok because I will stop soon. They promised I would, and I must believe them, because it means I am justified in my role as exterminator. When the termites are gone, and the eco-system is balanced once more... there will be Peace.

So, as I arrived upon the city – the city-of-four-hundred-thousand-souls – I looked to the button one more time. Can I do it again? Can I do it this one last time, for Peace?

My debate was answered before it had begun. If Peace was the reward, then I could do it- would do it... Or was it the precedent that decided I would? The knowledge that I had done it a hundred times before, why not again?

I thought to the dream. Light omitting from the rotten core...

The truth is, I still think dreams are dreams.

Bullet riddled hippos are bullet riddled hippos.

But I'm too far gone now.

And a chance for Peace is as much a dream as anything.

And so I press the button.

And a familiar mushroom rises to greet me.

Owen J.Wall grew up in Cheltenham, United Kingdom, spending most of his youth hopping between random interests and mostly short-lived obsessions. These ranged from housing ant colonies, to stop motion animations, to wildlife photography. The one relentless fascination was fiction writing, first emerging at the age of five. Fifteen years later, now a second-year creative writing student, he strives to get his stories out there, working daily across numerous creative projects. His interests lie in a range of genres, though his focus is on story and character. He would consider Stephen King to be his greatest influence.

https://twitter.com/BookNoggin

CATCHING MY BREATH

Jill Waters

Tyres crunched over the gravel of the car park and marram grass danced in the breeze. Ted watched as families played in the dunes and herring gulls swooped low, opportunistically seeking a snatched delicacy, stolen from an unsuspecting picnicker. 'You okay, love?' asked Michelle, watching as her husband leaned against the side of the car.

'Yes, fine. Just need...need to catch my breath.'

'We shouldn't have come. It's too soon. Let's get back in the car. I knew we shouldn't have come.' Putting the picnic back in the boot, she noticed her hands shaking.

Ted reached toward her. 'No. Wait. I'll be alright in a minute. I want to see the sea. It's been too long since I've seen the sea.'

'But it'll still be here tomorrow. And the next day. Maybe wait until you've got your strength back a bit. The doctor said...'

Ted looked at his wife, noticed her swallowing hard, but felt suddenly angry. 'I know what the doctor said. I was there, remember.'

'He said if you take care, there's no reason that...'

'I know. No reason I shouldn't last till this time next year. That's the point. I don't want to take care. I want to see the sea. If you won't come with me, I'll go on my own.' Bloody-mindedness and adrenalin kicked in and Ted stalked off, not caring if his wife followed.

'Wait... of course I'll come. Listen. I can hear the waves.' She ran to take her husband's arm. For a second he considered brushing her off, but, instead looked into her face and was wracked with guilt.

'Sorry, love. It's the medication. Makes me snarky. Didn't mean to snap at you.' he sighed, 'I just wish you could understand.'

Now Michelle's hackles rose. 'Understand what? That you want to ignore all sensible advice? That you want to carry on as if nothing has happened? I do try, you know, but I simply can't. I don't know why you seem so determined to leave me. The children.'

'That's not true. You know that's not what this is about.' Ahead the sea appeared, a sparkling jewel reaching toward the horizon. 'Ah, the sea. Beautiful.'

'It really is - seems to go on forever,' she paused, took a breath, 'So why won't you do what the doctors say?'

'What? Take it easy? Sit on a sofa and watch daytime TV?'

'Would that be so bad? We could get Netflix.'

'Sometimes I think you don't know me at all. When have I ever sat on my arse watching TV all day?'

'Ted, there's no need to be crude.'

'Sorry, Chelle, but when?' He pulled away, eyes fixed on the horizon, feeling himself get angrier with every word she said.

Failing to read his mood, she continued, 'Well things have changed. We're getting older. And the doctor said...well he said you need to take it easy.'

'Sod the doctors. I'm not ready to change,' his voice broke, 'I'm not ready for any of this.'

'Oh don't. You'll start me off. Look. There's a bench. Let's take the weight off. Have a rest. I need one even if you don't. I'll get us a coffee from the kiosk. Back in a bit.'

Ted sat alone, 'Oh, will you look at that view,' he said to no-one at all, 'I will never tire of it. I needed to smell the sea air, feel the heat of the sun on my face. Peace. Of mind. Of body.'

It didn't last long.

'I got you a decaff. Thought it best. Decaff latte, just one sugar. Do you need one of your pills?'

Again the anger swelled, 'For Christ's sake, Michelle. Leave it. I'm seventy-four. I do not want or need a bloody nursemaid. Can't we just enjoy the moment?'

'I don't think I'll ever enjoy a moment again,' she replied, tears in her eyes, 'You must know that I'm scared - just waiting in some sort of hideous purgatory.'

Ted looked at her. 'But it's me that's ill.'

'And that's why I'm scared. Don't you see? I need to be your nursemaid. To wrap you up in cotton wool. To protect you. It's what I do. What I've always done.'

Still staring out to sea, Ted almost whispered, 'But you can't protect me from this. Not forever. And you must see that if I let you do all those things, the person you're clinging to will die a long time before my stupid body does.'

'But I'm scared,' she repeated, staring at her feet.

'So am I, love, but the prospect of not living my life as I want is far scarier than the thought of actually dying.'

'I'm not sure I can handle it,' she said, turning towards him, 'I feel like I'll never have any peace.'

'And I'm truly sorry that my 'peace' comes at your expense. From days looking at the sea to nights at the pub quiz and a nice bottle of wine now and again, whether the doctor says it's okay or not. I need to find peace in the chaos of playing with Theo and Tilly, even if it exhausts me the next day, so my grandchildren remember good times with me. And if all that ultimately shortens my life, so be it.'

'Quality over quantity. That's quite the speech.' Despite herself, Michelle began to smile.

'Well, wouldn't you rather spend the time we have left creating memories? It has to be better than stagnating indoors to a background of Escape to the Country and Pointless'

'Hang on,' laughed Michelle, 'You like Pointless.'

Ted sensed he was winning the battle. Ironic really, a battle over whose 'peace' counted more. He stood and walked away, calling over his shoulder, 'Come on, the tide is turning. I think I'm ready for a paddle.'

'You're ruddy bonkers, you know that,' said Michelle, running after him.

'Probably,' said Ted. 'Come on - last one in buys the ice creams.'

> I retired from teaching six years ago, and use writing to keep my brain cells working. I have written blogs and a range of fiction, recently completing the first draft of a novel. When I'm not writing, I play tennis at my local club and make clothes for my grandchildren. I am a season ticket holder at Norwich City, so I also enjoy the odd glass of wine!
> www.instagram.com/landofthebluerinse